D0968720

THE CHRISTMAS
OF THE PHONOGRAPH RECORDS

The Christmas of the Phonograph Records

A Recollection

MARI SANDOZ

Illustrated by James W. Brown

UNIVERSITY OF NEBRASKA PRESS · LINCOLN

Library of Congress Catalog Card Number 66–19267

First printing December, 1966
Second printing March, 1967

Manufactured in the United States of America

THE CHRISTMAS
OF THE PHONOGRAPH RECORDS

It seems to me that I remember it all quite clearly. The night was very cold, footsteps squeaking in the frozen snow that had lain on for over two weeks, the roads in our region practically unbroken. But now the holidays were coming and wagons had pushed out on the long miles to the railroad, with men enough to scoop a trail for each other through the deeper drifts.

My small brother and I had been asleep in our attic bed long enough to frost the cover of the feather tick at our faces when there was a shouting in the road before the house, running steps, and then the sound of the broom handle thumping against the ceiling below us, and father booming out, "Get up! The phonograph is here!"

The phonograph! I stepped out on the coyote skin at our bed, jerked on my woolen stockings and my shoes, buttoning my dress as I slipped down the outside stairs in the fading moon.

Lamplight was pouring from the open door in a cloud of freezing mist over the back end of a loaded wagon, with three neighbors easing great boxes off, father limping back and forth shouting, "Don't break me my records!" his breath white around his dark beard.

Inside the house mother was poking sticks of wood into the firebox of the cookstove, her eyes meeting mine for a moment, shining, her concern about the extravagance of a talking machine when we needed overshoes for our chilblains apparently forgotten. The three largest boxes were edged through the doorway and filled much of the kitchen-living room floor. The neighbors stomped their felt boots at the stove and held their hands over the hot lids while father ripped at the boxes with his crowbar, the frozen nails squealing as they let go. First there was the machine, varnished oak, with a shining cylinder for the records, and then the horn, a great black, gilt-ribbed morning glory, and the crazy angled rod arm and chain to hold it in place.

By now a wagon full of young people from the Dutch community on Mirage Flats turned into

our yard. At a school program they had heard about the Edison phonograph going out to Old Jules Sandoz. They trooped in at our door, piled their wraps in the leanto and settled along the benches to wait.

Young Jule and James, the brothers next to me in age, were up too, and watching father throw excelsior aside, exposing a tight packing of round paper containers a little smaller than a middle-sized baking powder can, with more layers under these, and still more below. Father opened one and while I read out the instructions in my German-accented fifth-grade country school English, he slipped the brown wax cylinder on the machine, cranked the handle carefully, and set the needle down. Everybody waited, leaning forward. There was a rhythmic frying in the silence, and then a whispering of sound, soft and very, very far away.

It brought a murmur of disappointment and an escaping laugh, but gradually the whispers loudened into the sextet from *Lucia*, into what still seems to me the most beautiful singing in the world. We all clustered around, the visitors, fourteen, fifteen by now, and mother too, caught while pouring hot chocolate into cups, her long-handled pan still tilted in the air. Looking back I realize something of the meaning of the light in her face: the hunger for music she must have felt, coming from Switzerland, the country of music, to a western Nebraska government claim. True, we sang old country songs in the evenings, she leading, teaching us all she knew, but plainly it had not been enough, really nothing.

By now almost everybody pushed up to the boxes to see what there was to play, or called out some title hopefully. My place in this was established from the start. I was to run the machine, play the two-minute records set before me. There were violin pieces for father, among them *Alpine Violets* and *Mocking Bird* from the first box opened; *Any Rags*, *Red Wing*, and *I'm Trying so Hard to Forget You* for the young people; *Rabbit Hash* for my brothers, their own selection from the catalog; and Schubert's *Serenade* and *Die Kapelle* for mother, with almost everyone laughing over *Casey at the Telephone*, all except father. He claimed he could not understand such broken

English, he who gave even the rankest westernism a French pronunciation.

With the trail broken to the main bridge of the region, just below our house, and this Christmas Eve, there was considerable travel on the road, people passing most of the night. The lighted windows, the music, the gathering of teams and saddlehorses in the yard, and the sub-zero weather tolled them in to the weathered little frame house with its leanto.

"You better set more yeast. We will have to bake again tomorrow," mother told me as she cut into a *zopf*, one of the braids of coffee cake baked in tins as large as the circle of both her arms. This was the last of five planned to carry us into the middle of holiday week.

By now the phonograph had been moved to the top of the washstand in our parents' kalsomined bedroom, people sitting on the two double beds, on the round-topped trunk and on benches carried in, some squatting on their heels along the wall. The little round boxes stood everywhere, on the dresser and on the board laid from there to the washstand and on the window sills, with more brought in to be played and father still shouting over the music, "Don't break me my records!" Some were broken, the boxes slipping out of unaccustomed or cold-stiffened hands, the brown wax perhaps already cracked by the railroad.

When the Edison Military Band started a gay, blaring galop, mother looked in at the bedroom door, pleased. Then she noticed all the records spread out there, and in the kitchen-living room behind her, and began to realize their number. "Three hundred!" she exclaimed in German, speaking angrily in father's direction, "Looks to me like more than three thousand!"

Father scratched under his bearded chin, laughing slyly. "I added to the order," he admitted. He didn't say how many, nor that there were other brands besides the Edison here, including several hundred foreign recordings obtained through a Swiss friend in New York, at a stiff price.

Mother looked at him, her blue eyes tragic, as she could make them. "You paid nothing on the mortgage! All the twenty-one-hundred-dollar inheritance wasted on a talking machine!"

No, father denied, puffing at his corncob pipe. Not all. But mother knew him well. "You did not buy the overshoes for the children. You forgot everything except your stamp collection, your guns, and the phonograph!"

"The overshoes are coming. I got them cheaper on time, with the guns."

"More debts!" she accused bitterly, but before she could add to this one of the young Swiss, Maier perhaps, or Paul Freye, grabbed her and, against the stubbornness of her feet, whirled her back into the kitchen in the galop from the Edison band. He raced mother from door to stove and back again and around and around, so her blue calico skirts flew out and the anger died from her face. Her eyes began to shine in an excitement I had never seen in them, and I realize now, looking back, all the fun our mother missed in her working life, even in her childhood in the old country, and during the much harder years later.

That galop started the dancing. Hastily the table was pushed against the wall, boxes piled on top of it, the big ones dragged into the leanto. Waltzes, two-steps, quadrilles, and schottisches were sorted out and set in a row ready for me to play while one of the men shaved a candle over the kitchen floor. There was room for only one set of square dancers but our bachelor neighbor, Charley Sears, called the turns with enthusiasm. The Peters girls, two school teachers, and several other young women whom I've forgotten were well outnumbered by the men, as is common in new communities. They waltzed, two-stepped, formed a double line for a Bohemian polka, or schottisched around the room, one couple close behind the other to, perhaps, *It Blew, Blew, Blew.* Once Charley Sears grabbed my hand and drew me out to try a quadrille, towering over me as he swung me on the corner and guided me through the allemande left. My heart pounded in shyness and my home-made shoes compounded my awkwardness. Later someone else dragged me out into a two-step, saying, "Like this: 'one, two; one, two.' Just let yourself go."

Ah, so that was how it was done. Here started a sort of craze that was to hold me for over twenty years, through the bear dance, the turkey trot, the Charleston, and into the Lindy hop. But that first night with the records even Old Jules had to try a round polka, even with his foot crippled in a long-ago well accident. When he took his pipe out of his mouth, dropped it lighted into his pocket, and whirled mother around several times we knew that this was a special occasion. Before this we had never seen him even put an arm around her.

After the boys had heard their selection again, and *The Preacher and the Bear*, they fell asleep on the floor and were carried to their bed in the leanto. Suddenly I remembered little Fritzlie alone in the attic, perhaps half-frozen. I hurried up the slippery, frosted steps. He was crying, huddled together under the feather tick, cold and afraid, deserted by the cat too, sleeping against the warm chimney. I brought the boy down, heavy hulk that he was, and laid him in with his brothers. By then the last people started to talk of leaving, but the moon had clouded over, the night-dark roads winding and treacherous through the drifts. Still, those who had been to town must get home with the Christmas supplies and such presents as they could manage for their children when they awoke in the morning.

Toward dawn father dug out *Sempach*, a song of a heroic Swiss battle, in which one of mother's ancestors fell, and *Andreas Hofer*, of another national hero. Hiding her pleasure at these records, mother hurried away to the cellar under the house for two big hams, one to boil while the Canada goose roasted for the Christmas dinner. From the second ham she sliced great red rounds for the frying pan and I mixed up a triple batch of baking powder biscuits and set on the two-gallon coffee pot. When the sun glistened on the frosted snow, the last of the horses huddled together in our yard were on the road. By then some freighters forced to camp out by an upset wagon came whipping their teams up the icy pitch from the Niobrara River and stopped in. Father was slumped in his chair, letting his pipe fall into his beard, but he looked up and recognized the men as from a ranch accused of driving out bona fide settlers. Instead of rising to order them off the place he merely said "How!" in the Plains greeting, and dropped back into his doze. Whenever the music stopped noticeably, he lifted his shaggy head, complaining, "Can't you keep the machine

going?" even if I had my hands in the biscuits. "Play the *Mocking Bird* again," he might order, or a couple of the expensive French records of pieces he had learned to play indifferently in the violin lessons of his boyhood in Neuchatel. He liked *Spring Song* too, and *La Paloma*, an excellent mandolin rendition of *Come ye Disconsolate*, and several German love songs he had learned from his sweetheart, in Zurich, who had not followed him to America.

Soon my three brothers were up again and calling for their favorites as they settled to plates of ham with red gravy and biscuits, Fritzlie from the top of two catalogs piled on a chair shouting too, just to be heard. None of them missed the presents that we never expected on Christmas; besides, what could be finer than the phonograph?

While mother fed our few cattle and the hogs I worked at the big stack of dishes with one of the freighters to wipe them. Afterward I got away to the attic and slept a little, the music from below faint through my floating of dreams. Suddenly I awoke, remembering what day this was and that young Jule and I had hoped father might go cottontail hunting in the canyons up the river and help us drag home a little pine tree. Christmas had become a time for a tree, even without presents, a tree and singing, with at least one new song learned.

I dressed and hurried down. Father was asleep and there were new people in the bedroom and in the kitchen too, talking about the wonder of the music rolling steadily from the big horn. In our Swiss way we had prepared for the usual visitors during the holidays, with family friends on Christmas and surely some of the European homeseekers father had settled on free land, as well as passersby just dropping in to get warm and perhaps be offered a cup of coffee or chocolate or a glass of father's homemade wine if particularly privileged. Early in the forenoon the Syrian peddler we called Solomon drew up in the yard with his high four-horse wagon. I remember him every time I see a picture of Krishna Menon—the tufted hair, the same lean yellowish face and long white teeth. Solomon liked to strike our place for Christmas because there might be customers around and besides there was no display of religion to make him uncomfortable in his Mohammedanism, father said, although one might run into a stamp-collecting priest or a hungry preacher at our house almost any other time.

So far as I know, Solomon was the first to express what others must have thought. "Excuse it please, Mrs. Sandoz," he said, in the polite way of peddlers, "but it seem to uneducated man like me the new music is for fine palace—"

Father heard him. "Nothing's too good for my family and my neighbors," he roared out.

"The children have the frozen feet—" the man said quietly.

"Frozen feet heal! What you put in the mind lasts!"

The peddler looked down into his coffee cup, half full of sugar, and said no more.

It was true that we had always been money poor and plainly would go on so, but there was plenty of meat and game, plenty of everything that the garden, the young orchard, the field, and the open country could provide, and for all of which there was no available market. Our bread, dark and heavy, was from our hard macaroni wheat ground at a local water mill. The hams, sausage, and bacon were from our own smokehouse, the cellar full of our own potatoes, barrels of pickles and sauerkraut, and hundreds of jars of canned fruit and vegetables, crocks of jams and jellies, wild and tame, including buffalo berry, that wonderful, tart, golden-red jelly from the silvery bush that seems to retreat before close settlement much like the buffalo and the whooping crane. Most of the root crops were in a long pit outside, and the attic was strung with little sacks of herbs and poppy seed, bigger ones of dried green beans, sweetcorn, chokecherries, sandcherries, and wild plums. Piled along the low sides of the attic were bushel bags of popcorn, peas, beans, and lentils, the flour stacked in rows with room between for the mousing cat.

Sugar, coffee, and chocolate were practically all we bought for the table, with perhaps a barrel of blackstrap molasses for cookies and brown cake, all laid in while the fall roads were still open.

When the new batch of coffee cake was done and the fresh bread and buns, the goose in the oven, we took turns getting scrubbed at the heater

in the leanto, and put on our best clothes, mostly made-over from some adult's but well-sewn. Finally we spread mother's two old country linen cloths over the table lengthened out by boards laid on salt barrels for twenty-two places. While mother passed the platters, I fed the phonograph with records that Mrs. Surber and her three musical daughters had selected, soothing music: Bach, Mozart, Brahms, and the *Moonlight Sonata* on two foreign records that father had hidden away so they would not be broken, along with an a capella *Stille Nacht* and some other foreign ones mother wanted saved. For lightness, Mrs. Surber had added *The Last Rose of Summer*, to please Elsa, the young soprano soon to be a professional singer in Cleveland, and a little Strauss and Puccini, while the young people wanted Ada Jones and *Monkey Land* by Collins and Harlan.

There was stuffed Canada goose with the buffalo berry jelly; ham boiled in a big kettle in the leanto; watercress salad; chow-chow and pickles, sweet and sour; dried green beans cooked with bacon and a hint of garlic; carrots, turnips, mashed potatoes and gravy, with coffee from the start to the pie, pumpkin and gooseberry. At the dishpan set on the high water bench, where I had to stand on a little box for comfort, the dishes were washed as fast as they came off the table, with a relay of wipers. There were also waiting young men and boys to draw water from the bucket well, to chop stove wood and carry it in.

As I recall now, there were people at the table for hours. A letter of mother's says that the later uninvited guests got sausage and sauerkraut, squash, potatoes, and fresh bread, with canned plums and cookies for dessert. Still later there was a big roaster full of beans and side-meat brought in by a lady homesteader, and some mince pies made with wild plums to lend tartness instead of apples, which cost money.

All this time there was the steady stream of music and talk from the bedroom. I managed to slip in the *Lucia* a couple of times until a tart-tongued woman from over east said she believed I was getting addled from all that hollering. We were not allowed to talk back to adults, so I put on the next record set before me, this one *Don't Get Married Any More, Ma*, selected for a visiting

Chicago widow looking for her fourth husband, or perhaps her fifth. Mother rolled her eyes up at this bad taste, but father and the other old timers laughed over their pipes.

We finally got mother off to bed in the attic for her first nap since the records came. Downstairs the floor was cleared and the Surber girls showed their dancing-school elegance in the waltzes. There was a stream of young people later in the afternoon, many from the skating party at the bridge. Father, red-eyed like the rest of us, limped among them, soaking up their praise, their new respect. By this time my brothers and I had given up having a tree. Then a big boy from up the river rode into the yard dragging a pine behind his horse. It was a shapely tree, and small enough to fit on a box in the window, out of the way. The youth was the son of father's worst enemy, the man who had sworn in court that Jules Sandoz shot at him, and got our father thirty days in jail, although everybody, including the judge, knew that Jules Sandoz was a crack shot and what he fired at made no further appearances.

As the son came in with the tree, someone

announced loudly who he was. I saw father look toward his Winchester on the wall, but he was not the man to quarrel with an enemy's children. Then he was told that the boy's father himself was in the yard. Now Jules Sandoz paled above his bearding, paled so the dancers stopped, the room silent under the suddenly foolish noise of the big-horned machine. Helpless, I watched father jump toward the rifle. Then he turned, looked to the man's gaunt-faced young son.

"Tell your old man to come in. We got some good Austrian music."

So the man came in, and sat hunched over near the door. Father had left the room, gone to the leanto, but after a while he came out, said his "How!" to the man, and paid no attention when Mrs. Surber pushed me forward to make the proper thanks for the tree that we were starting to trim as usual. We played *The Blue Danube* and some other pieces long forgotten now for the man, and passed him the coffee and *küchli* with the others. He tasted the thin flaky frycakes. "Your mother is a good cook," he told me. "A fine woman."

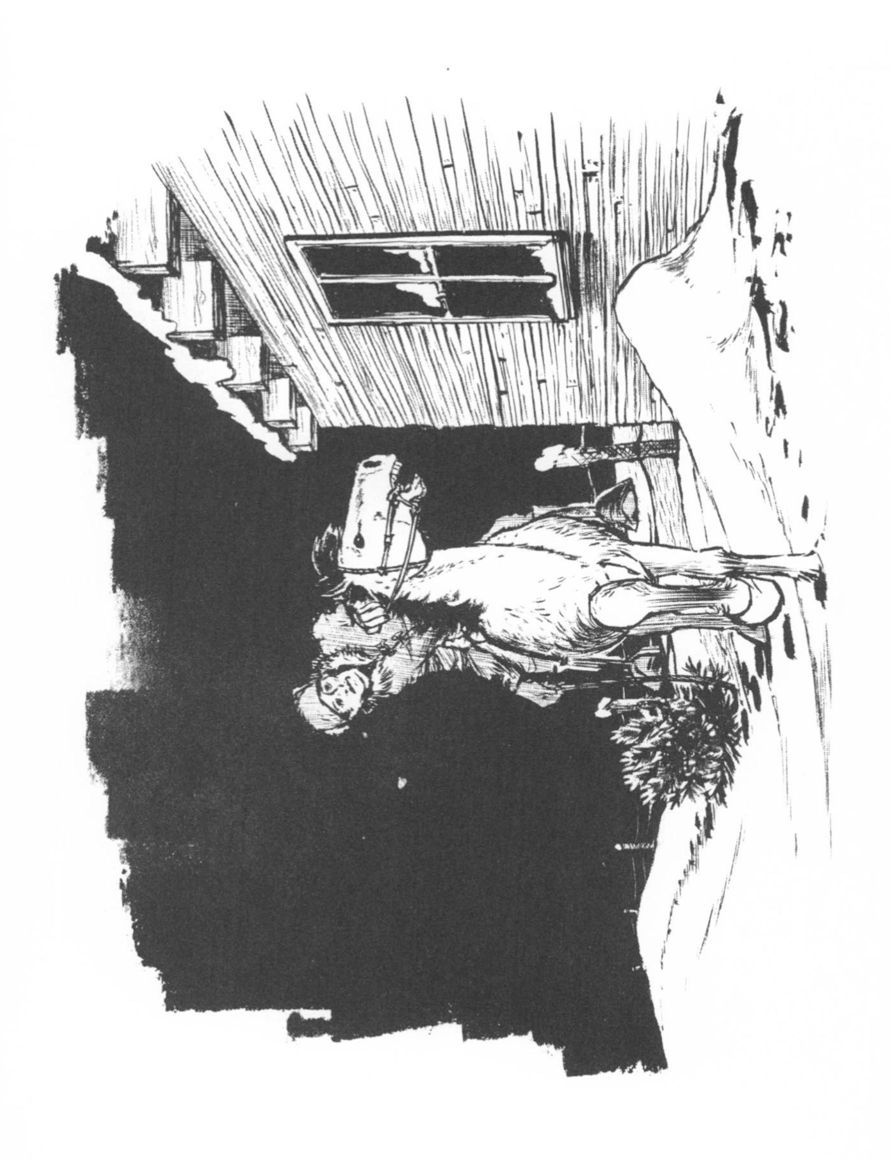

When he left with the skaters all of father's friends began to talk at once, fast, relieved. "You could have shot him down, on your own place, and not got a day in the pen for it," one said.

Old Jules nodded. "I got no use for his whole outfit, but the music is for everybody."

As I recall now, perhaps half a dozen of us, all children, worked at the tree, looping my strings of red rose hips and popcorn around it, hanging the people and animal cookies with chokecherry eyes, distributing the few Christmas tree balls and the tinsel and candleholders that the Surbers had given us several years before. I brought out the boxes of candles I had made by dipping string in melted tallow, and then we lit the candles and with my schoolmates I ran out into the cold of the road to look. The tree showed fine through the glass.

Now I had to go to bed, although the room below me was alive with dancing and I remembered that Jule and I had not sung our new song, *Amerika ist ein schönes Land* at the tree.

Holiday week was much like Christmas, the house full of visitors as the news of the fine music and the funny records spread. People appeared from fifty, sixty miles away and farther so long as the new snow held off, for there was no other such collection of records in all of western Nebraska, and none with such an open door. There was something for everybody, Irishmen, Scots, Swedes, Danes, Poles, Czechs as well as the Germans and the rest, something pleasant and nostalgic. The greatest variety in tastes was among the Americans, from *Everybody Works but Father*, *Arkansas Traveler*, and *Finkelstein at the Seashore* to love songs and the sentimental *Always in the Way*; from home and native region pieces to the patriotic and religious. They had strong dislikes too, even in war songs. One settler, a GAR veteran, burst into tears and fled from the house at the first notes of *Tenting Tonight*. Perhaps it was the memories it awakened. Many Americans were as interested in classical music as any European, and it wasn't always a matter of cultivated taste. One illiterate little woman from down the river cried with joy at Rubinstein's *Melody in F*.

"I has heard me talkin' and singin' before," she said apologetically as she wiped her eyes, "but I wasn't knowin' there could be something sweet as that come from a horn."

Afternoons and evenings, however, were still the time for the dancers. Finally it was New Year, the day when the Sandoz relatives, siblings, uncles and cousins, gathered, perhaps twenty of them immigrants brought in by the land locater, Jules. This year they were only a sort of eddy in the regular stream of outsiders. Instead of nostalgic jokes and talk of the family and the old country, there were the records to hear, particularly the foreign ones, and the melodies of the old violin lessons that the brothers had taken, and the guitar and mandolin of their one sister. Jules had to endure a certain amount of joking over the way he spent most of his inheritance. One brother was building a cement block home in place of his soddy with his, and a greenhouse. The sister was to have a fine large barn instead of a new home because her husband believed that next year Halley's comet would bring the end of the world. Ferdinand, the youngest of the brothers, had put his money into wild-cat oil stock and planned to become very wealthy.

Although most of their talk was in French, which mother did not speak, they tried to make up for this by complimenting her on the excellence of her chocolate and her golden fruit cake. Then they were gone, hot bricks at their feet, and calling back their adieus from the freezing night. It was a good thing they left early, mother told me. She had used up the last of the chocolate, the last cake of the two twenty-five pound caddies. We had baked up two sacks of flour, forty-nine pounds each, in addition to all that went into the Christmas preparations before the phonograph came. Three-quarters of a hundred pound bag of coffee had been roasted, ground, and used during the week, and all the winter's sausage and ham. The floor of the kitchen-living room, old and worn anyway, was much thinner for the week of dancing. New Year's night a man who had been there every day, all week, tilted back on one of the kitchen chairs and went clear through the floor.

"Oh, the fools!" father shouted at us all. "Had to wear out my floor dancing!"

But plainly he was pleased. It was a fine story to

tell for years, all the story of the phonograph records. He was particularly gratified by the praise of those who knew something about music, people like the Surbers and a visitor from a Czech community, a relative of Dvorak, the great composer. The man wrote an item for the papers, saying, "This Jules Sandoz has not only settled a good community of home-seekers, but is enriching their cultural life with the greatest music of the world."

"Probably wants to borrow money from you," mother said. "He has come to the wrong door."

Gradually the records for special occasions and people were stored in the leanto. For those used regularly, father and a neighbor made a lot of flat boxes to fit under the beds, always handy, and a cabinet for the corner at the bedroom door. The best, the finest from both the Edison and the foreign recordings, were put into this cabinet, with a door that didn't stay closed. One warmish day when I was left alone with the smaller children, the water pail needed refilling. I ran out to draw a bucket from the well. It was a hard and heavy pull for a growing girl and I hated it, always afraid that I wouldn't last, and would have to let the rope slip and break the windlass.

Somehow, in my uneasy hurry, I left the door ajar. The wind blew it back and when I had the bucket started up the sixty-five foot well, our big old sow, loose in the yard, pushed her way into the house. Horrified, I shouted to Fritzlie to get out of her way, but I had to keep pulling and puffing until the bucket was at the top. Then I ran in. Fritzlie was up on a chair, safe, but the sow had knocked down the record cabinet and scattered the cylinders over the floor. Standing among them as in corn, she was chomping down the wax records that had rolled out of the boxes, eating some, box and all. Furiously I thrashed her out with the broom, amidst squealings and shouts. Then I tried to save what I could. The sow had broken at least thirty or thirty-five of the best records and eaten all or part of twenty more. *La Paloma* was gone, and *Traumerei* and *Spring Song*; *Evening Star* too, and half of the *Moonlight*

Sonata and many others, foreign and domestic, including all of Brahms.

I got the worst whipping of my life for my carelessness, but the loss of the records hurt more, and much, much longer.